The Arrival

This Book Belongs to:

_____

CLANDESTINE ACTION AGENT

SECURITY CLEARANCE LEVEL: ALPHA

Battery: The Arrival

An ACTIONOPOLIS Book

Presented by Agent of D.A.N.G.E.R.

AGENT OF DANGER

KOMIKWERKS

Published by Komikwerks, LLC
1 Ruth Street
Worcester, MA 01602

Cover Illustration by Billy King
Edited by Shannon Eric Denton
Book Design by Kristen Fitzner Denton

ISBN-13: 978-1-933925-67-7
ISBN: 1-933925-67-1

When Adventure Is Your Destination!

The Arrival

Dedication

For Krysten, who inspired Kaia and who has inspired me since she was five years old.

— M.M.

TABLE OF CONTENTS

By Marc Mason

Created by

Shannon Eric Denton

and Marc Mason

When Adventure Is Your Destination!

Chapter 1
ARRIVAL MINUS 4 HOURS:
THE LIBRARY

Designate 5309 glided gently through the sterile hallway, keeping to the shadows where his natural color presented him camouflage. Pressing against the wall, he made his way to the door at the end, arriving without a sound. For long, agonizing minutes, he waited, making sure that no one else was nearby, until he could finally wait no more. Then he began breaking the sacred laws of Katahdin Prime.

First, he began manipulating his shape. He reached for the panel that locked and unlocked the door and allowed his hand to flow through its cracks and into the door's interior. Beings of his caste were expressly forbidden from altering their shape or anything about their appearance; the low were meant to be the low, in status and in look, and nothing was to change that. But 5309 had a natural curiosity that could not be stopped. He began practicing the changing of his shape two cycles prior, and now he was seeing his efforts come to fruition. He felt the circuits and tumblers that activated the door and activated them, and immediately, it unsealed with a hiss and opened to his touch.

5309 entered the room cautiously. Perhaps the shape manipulation could be forgiven, albeit with harsh punishment, but what he was about to do was considered an act of highest treason. Crossing this threshold meant there was to be no turning back. Yet he did so anyway. The door sealed shut behind him as he stared in wonder at the data terminals flashing all around him. Each one carried a symbol for what they contained: history, technology, science, education, literature… for a moment he felt overwhelmed. Then he began defying every tenet of

Katahdin social structure.

From the moment 5309 first gained awareness, the rules governing the lower caste were repeatedly explained to him, and those rules were fairly simple: you are low and will always be low; you will be given tasks to help maintain society within The City of High; if you fail in your tasks or attempt to work above or outside your caste, you will be punished.

It was early in his existence that 5309 realized he was not like others in his caste. It began when he asked questions about his assigned tasks, and it grew when he came to the conclusion that those in higher castes were in possession of knowledge that those of low caste did not. In violation of all social norms, 5309 decided that this was not acceptable.

5309 wanted more.

Now, within the walls of this remote data library, more was within his grasp. 5309 activated the nearest data terminal and began accessing the knowledge within. It was the most glorious experience of his existence; the gift before him, the ability to read and learn new things that had been denied him both excited 5309 and gave him a sense of sadness. He knew – knew – that the information he was seeing would, if widely disseminated, change the entire social structure of Katahdin Prime.

Perhaps that was what was needed. Perhaps that was to be 5309's purpose.

Time passed, and 5309 lost track of his own movements as he visited terminal after terminal, gaining dangerous, forbidden knowledge. He forgot about everything outside of the library, his focus absolute. Unfortunately, he forgot about performing his assigned tasks.

5309 was late. Very late.

This he was blissfully unaware of until a series of alarms rang out within the library. The staccato sound, accompanied by flashing orange lights, startled 5309 out of his reverie. Suddenly understanding that he had made a horrific mistake, he disconnected from the data terminal and started moving in the direction of the door. However, as he did, he heard it open and voices began to echo throughout the library. Stopping, 5309 moved to a position where he could take a quick look at the door.

It was his worst fears come true: four Togai stood at the entrance to the library.

The Togai, warrior race, the strong right arm of the high caste. Their sole reason to exist was to track, capture, and punish criminals… fatally punish criminals. 5309 considered various scenarios in his mind, and none of them were promising. The excitement he had been feeling only short moments before was now gone, replaced by fear for his very existence.

It was all too likely that 5309's revolution was over before it had truly begun.

Chapter 2
ARRIVAL MINUS 3 HOURS:
THE TRUCK

The taunts echoed through the school corridor as Kaia walked away. Cutting words about her Hopi heritage, about her shyness, about her intelligence, about her looks… nothing seemed to be off limits to her oppressors. She anticipated being bullied when he mom remarried and they moved from the reservation to the city, but the level of nastiness never failed to shock her. She knew it wasn't everyone at the school but this select group of bullies were so mean it seemed like it at times.

As she exited outside, she was met on the front steps by Danny Gray, her only friend in what she was rapidly beginning to consider a form of prison. "Hey, Kaia!" he said too loudly. The young boy was deaf in his left ear and he wore a hearing aid in his right. He worked hard every day to sound normal when he spoke, but occasionally his volume control was not brilliant. "Get away clean?"

"Nope. Got an earful with every step. Very thorough. They must have wanted to make sure they ruined my weekend."

"Ugh. Sorry."

She stopped and looked down. "I know you'll say I don't really mean it, but I envy you. You can turn off that thing in your ear and never hear a word of it." She reflected for a moment. "And considering some of the things I've heard them say about you, you should be grateful."

Danny shook his head. "But when you get past those jerks… Kaia, I would love to hear the world in stereo again."

"I know." She started walking toward the bike rack. "I'll call you as soon as I know what verdict the 'rents drop about tonight."

Kaia walked into the kitchen, and much to her surprise, both her mother and step-father were sitting at the table. They were playing cards and smiling at one another, and though Kaia had not been thrilled to move to Ahwautukee, it was clear that Don Etchell was absolutely in love with her mother. She had never seen Graham Little look at her mother like that; her father was an emotionally stoic man, rarely showing affection to either Kaia or her mom Lilith. Seeing how Don treated Lilith, Kaia had little doubt why her parents had split. She simply wished it hadn't led them to a school system where every day was an exercise in trying not to go ballistic and defend herself against incessant name calling.

"Hi honey!" Lilith said with a bright smile. "How was your day?"

"Don't ask," Kaia replied. She poured herself a glass of apple juice and began drinking.

"The jerk squad again?" Don asked. "I know you said not to, but really… why not let us call the school and have them do something about it?"

Kaia put the cup down and sighed. "Because it would just make things worse. That would make me look weak… they already think I'm weak. But I won't show them that it's true. I won't."

He held up his hands in a show of submission. "Okay, okay… you win." Don winked at Lilith. "I admire that you want to stand your ground."

"Some days, I would give just about anything to be a little girl back on the rez, sitting on Grandma's lap and listening to her stories about the old days. At least there I'm not as much of a freak."

"We know," Lilith said. "So we feel like maybe a reward is due for you sticking it out the way you have." Don reached into his pocket and pulled out his keys. Smiling, he slid them across the table to Kaia.

"Seriously?" she asked, astonished.

Don nodded at her. "Take the truck. Pick up Danny, go to Casa Grande and see your telescope. Just remember: if you become an astronomer, you have to name a planet after your mom and me."

"Major, you asked me to report if I saw anything

unusual during the field generation for the telescope."
The young scientist, deeply intimidated by Major
Stewart, was almost quivering in his shoes. "Well,
umm, sir, I've spotted something odd."

Stewart rose from his desk until his six and a half
foot frame filled the room. "Define 'odd', son."

The scientist cleared his throat. "I've tracked
several fluctuations in the central integrity field. Like
the frequency of the field is locking onto something
momentarily and then letting go."

"Theories?"

"That's the best I've got."

Stewart cocked an eyebrow. "Danger?"

"Unknown."

The Major thought for a moment, then exhaled.
"Keep and eye on it. For now, we stay on schedule."

"Yessir."

As he watched the scientist walk away, the
Major grabbed an antacid off of his desk and began
chewing it. "One more thing that could go wrong.
Fantastic," he thought. "I should have just retired."

Chapter 3
ARRIVAL MINUS 2 HOURS:
THE CHASE

5309 dodged an energy blast, the red bolt missing him by mere microns as it passed by. The Togai warrior who fired it – known only as 84A - growled in anger and began pursuing 5309 again as he waited for his weapon to recharge. This was, the Togai noted, not what should be happening.

For as long as he had drawn breath, he had been told of the weakness of the low caste. How all they were good for was to perform menial tasks. And for those who stepped out of line, though it was rarely someone of the low, they were easy prey for the great warriors of the Togai. Yet this one, Designate 5309, had proven to be the exception to all his training. Though a member of the low, he was demonstrating cleverness on a scale not seen in that caste. This 5309 had also been illegally practicing the alteration of his form into various shapes, something that even the Togai were generally discouraged from doing.

Indeed, the Togai were trained to use their own inner energies – their core being – to charge their swords with power and fire energy bolts from them. Manipulation of form only came if they were merged with a secondary power source, and that had not happened to anyone during 84A's lifespan.

As 84A continued his chase, he shouted at 5309. "You are a fool, low! You run from the inevitable!" The dark figure of 5309 did not even turn to stop or respond. Instead, 84A's quarry weaved his way through the central records building in what the Togai felt assured was a ridiculous denial of the punishment that was required for the crimes that had been committed. Annoyed, he continued to follow, waiting for his sword to recharge and silently hoping that one of his brethren was somewhere ahead. If procedure was being followed correctly – and the Togai never failed to follow procedure – 84A was running 5309 into a trap from which escape would be impossible. Then, and only then, could 84A rest.

Danny climbed into the truck's cab. "Wow. I almost can't believe it. They actually gave you the keys!"

"Which means we get to have an epic evening of stargazing and astronomy coolness." Kaia couldn't stop herself from smiling at the thought.

"Your folks must have really wanted some romantic alone time," Danny said, his eyes staring off into the horizon.

Kaia's head snapped around. "Can we please pretend that isn't true so I don't vomit?"

He shrugged at her. "Don't be a hater."

She sighed. "Anyway, the on-site museum has one last tour that we can make, and at the end, they let you watch the dish being moved into position from the observation deck. After that, they kick you out, but you can apparently watch from afar or whatever."

"Which we will."

"Absolutely!" Kaia looked wistful for a moment. "I can't even begin to tell you, Danny... the sky out on the rez... it's amazeballs. No light pollution, just pure starlight. The universe served up on a platter."

Danny grinned at the thought. "I hope I can see it some day."

"I'll take you out there sometime." She got lost in a memory. "When I was a little girl, like five years old, I saw a movie about a female scientist who works for SETI. She winds up getting a signal from outer space and gets to be the first person to meet alien life."

"Awesome."

Kaia nodded. "Inspirational. I mean... this is the stuff I've been chasing my whole life since, and now it's thirty minutes from my house. How cool is that?"

"Mega-cool," Danny agreed.

Chapter 4
ARRIVAL MINUS 1 HOUR:
ANCIENT ASTRONAUTS

The tour was over, but Kaia and Danny did not walk toward the door to the observation deck. "Not yet," Kaia whispered to Danny as the group began moving to the final destination. Instead, she stopped them short, holding her place in front of the relic in front of her.

"It kills me not to be able to touch it," she said, waiving her hand at the Apollo capsule in front of them. "Ugh. I want to go inside! See what they saw, sit where they sat!"

Danny nodded. "That would be sweeeeeeeeet."

She smiled at the idea. "Back then, those guys… ridiculously brave. Ancient technology got these guys to the moon, do you realize that? These days, no sane person would get on an airplane without wifi –"

"Bit of an exaggeration."

Kaia ignored him. "But these guys left orbit with baling wire and chewing gum. Their computer only had text features on it, too. No icons."

"The dark ages."

"Yeah. Best relic ever, right?"

He gave her a thumbs up. "Right." Danny gestured upward. "Observation deck?" Kaia spun around and started walking quickly to catch up with the tour group, Danny following close behind.

Major Stewart put his phone on speaker and continued talking. "I don't like it, I'll tell you that for free. When you're working with the kind of advanced tech this project is using –"

The voice on the other end crackled. "With this

kind of advanced tech, oddities are to be expected, Major. We've looked over the data you sent, and find no reason to postpone fully powering up the dish."

"Well. It's easy to be confident when you're sitting in Houston and not here," Stewart replied, his upper lip curling into a sneer. "But I've got live people here depending on me to make the right decision, and that includes civilians."

A long pause filled the air, the speaker hissing. After a moment, the voice reappeared. "Keep us posted about any changes, Major. Until then, proceed." An abrupt click ended the call, and Stewart pounded his desk in frustration.

Reaching into a nearby drawer, he pulled out a folder labeled S.E.T.I. ALPHA-5: TOP SECRET. Being careful, he spread the contents out on his desk, looking at the papers and drawings regarding the installation he had been given command of only months ago. Scanning thoroughly, he found the briefing abstract and began reading it again:

The dish represents a massive leap forward in our ability to scan for life in the cosmos. Beyond sending radar signals into the void, it also has a Heisenberg Displacement Generator built into it. Simply put, the dish can punch a hole into space; somewhere on the far side of the universe, the signal then punches out, allowing us to see further across the universe than ever before. S.E.T.I ALPHA-5 is the most technologically advanced piece of equipment ever created for this kind of work.

Stewart rubbed his temples. The central integrity field was generated by the Heisenberg component, the idea being that when the Heisenberg generator would open a hole in space on the other side of the universe and send the dish's signal through, the field needed to be steady on this end to prevent problems with space tearing apart…"or something like that," Stewart thought.

The older man exhaled. "So why is the field glitching like a sweater caught on a doorknob?"

Walking to his window, he looked out at the observation deck at the civilians who had come to see the dish go active. "Poor saps just think it's a radar installation," he muttered, "no idea we're messing with the fabric of the universe. Heh." The dish began to move on its axis, the boys down in the control room showing off for the visitors, as well as for themselves. Finally, when it was done, the people were escorted out of the building and to their vehicles.

"In the old days, I might have fired my gun into the air in celebration, but these days, you never know where the bullet will land. Bah," he groused. Suddenly, his eyes snapped open. "Oh my God!"

It was obvious to him now. Against astronomical odds, the signal on the far end was pinging against something, not just arriving in empty space! He raced from his office, praying he would reach the control room in time to stop the generator from being brought fully online.

Major Stewart was, unfortunately, thirty seconds too late.

Chapter 5
ARRIVAL

Kaia shifted the truck into 'drive' and began heading out of the parking lot. "That was SO cool. Totally next gen stuff."

"Yeah! All that tech surrounding the dish was pretty sweet. It moved seriously smooth, amiright?" Danny fidgeted with his seatbelt. "I expected it to be clunky. Maybe make grinding sounds or something."

"And the hum…" Kaia looked wistful for a moment. "Like the whole universe was vibrating. I can still hear it a bit."

"That makes one of us."

"Sorry." She turned onto a dirt road at the far end of the installation. "I think if we park out here, we can watch the dish move and scan, and we are far enough away that when the sun fully sets, we'll get an amazing sky."

Danny nodded in agreement. "Sweet."

5309 glided around a corner and found himself in a large, empty atrium. Brightly lit from all angles, his body, comprised of ebony energy, stood out. There was nowhere to hide here, he quickly realized. Looking around, he saw three other corridors branching away. He raced for the nearest one, but as he neared it, he saw a Togai moving swiftly toward him. Changing course, he went for the next one, but another Togai emerged to block his way. Knowing that he was likely doomed, he turned to look at the third, only to see a Togai warrior enter the atrium from it as well.

Panicked, 5309 fled to the center of the room, just as the Togai who had been chasing him made his entrance. He was now surrounded.

The Togai moved in unison, forming up and setting positions. 5309 came to the final realization that he had no options; there was nowhere else to run. He clinched his fists and closed his eyes, thinking about how disappointed the others from his crèche would be to hear of his crimes and his final fate. Re-opening his eyes, he spun in a slow circle, watching as the Togai charged their swords. The terrifying weapons throbbed and glowed bright red, and the Togai raised and pointed them at 5309.

"Designate 5309, for your crimes of sedition, violation of social norms, and resistance, you have been found guilty and sentenced to oblivion." 84A's words were dry and passionless, and tired of pursuing this deviant, he nodded to his comrades a silent count. But before they could complete their duties, the very atmosphere in the atrium seemed to explode.

ZZZZZZZZRRRRRRKKKKKKKKKKK!

5309 and the Togai were knocked to the floor as energy cascaded through the room. Blinking and shivering, 5309 lifted his head and saw what he could only describe as a tear in the air. A disc of crackling white energy was floating above him, and as 5309 regained his footing, one of the Togai fired his sword's energies, missing 5309 and hitting the disc, where it simply disappeared.

The other Togai began to come around as well, and 5309 made a snap decision. His existence was over if he stayed in the atrium… if he stayed on Katahdin Prime. But the disc had sent the Togai's blast somewhere else. A decision was made, and for the first time since he began his life as a criminal, 5309 spoke:

"I have nothing to lose and everything to gain."

To the shock of the Togai, 5309 leapt into the tear in the air and vanished.

Kaia and Danny sat in the back of the truck, their backs against the cab. He reached into a cooler and handed her a can of soda, which she opened and took a drink from. Suddenly, she cocked an eyebrow and looked quizzically into the distance. "Huh. That's interesting."

"What? The root beer? I thought that was your brand."

She shook her head. "The soda's great. No, I mean that the hum just picked up. A lot." Kaia held up her hand. "I know you can't hear it. Not trying to rub it in, I promise. What I mean is that it feels like they just upped the power output back at the dish, and in a huge way."

"So? Maybe they kept in on low until the civilians were away for safety purposes."

"I guess. Probably completely normal. I mean, what do I know? I've never seen one of these up close before. Science is –"

"Kaia…"

"tricky." She continued. "I can't wait to get some astrophysics classes in college. That should –"

"KAIA!" Danny's tone cut her off. "It's my first time, too, so pardon me for asking: is that normal?"

The kids stared at the radar dish, watching intently as strange sparks of lightning began crackling around it. Kaia was baffled; there was no weather in the area to speak of. Yet these strange sparks were randomly appearing throughout the sky.

"Umm, no…" she said, unable to stop watching.

He cleared his throat. "I don't want to be a drag, but those sparks seem to be moving further away from the dish."

"And lasting longer," Kaia added.

"Maybe we ought to go?"

"Maybe…" She stood and hopped down to the ground. "I hate the idea of missing anything tho –

"BZZZZZZRRRRRRRKKKKKKKKKKK!

Coughing and wheezing, Kaia and Danny picked themselves up and were transfixed by what appeared to be a hole in the air. A disc of white energy floated a few feet above them.

"Kaia, are you okay?" Danny wiped blood away from his nose. "Kaia?"

She stood transfixed, staring intently at the crackling energies above her head. Suddenly, the center of the disc turned dark, and the darkness seemed to be growing. In her mind, she tried to move, but terror gripped her body and she was frozen in place. Then, without warning, an ebony figure erupted from the disc and landed on Kaia.

Danny screamed, but only briefly. The same could not be said for the screams of Kaia and 5309. Their screams went on for a long, long time.

Chapter 6
ARRIVAL PLUS 5 MINUTES:
MEETING OF THE MINDS

Kaia struggled to open her eyes. Slowly, her eyelids fluttered, the passing seconds bringing her close to full awareness. However, as she did, the awareness was not joined by anything but pure darkness. No matter which way she turned her head, there was blackness… seemingly infinite in every direction. The budding young scientist attempted to wrap her mind around what was happening – what she had seen, her immediate and overwhelming panic – but nothing she had covered in her studies had prepared her for anything she was experiencing at that moment. Finally, she drew the only conclusion she could:

"Oh, no... I've gone blind. Please, God, let it be temporary. Danny! Danny, are you there?"

Designate 'Danny' unknown. The voice echoed, and Kaia felt her hands and knees begin to quiver. Self is designate 5309. 5309 responds to inquiry: upon electrochemical download of language center and diagnostic scan of biological systems, 5309 verifies that no loss of vision has taken place in biological unit designated 'Kaia Little'.

She clinched her fists and flexed her knees, attempting to regain control of herself. "Who are you? Where am I? Why can't I see?" She wiped away a tear from her right eye. "In case you haven't noticed, I'm kinda freakin' out!"

Two shimmering yellow eyes appeared out of the darkness, followed by a small mouth. As they approached, Kaia could see the slim outline of a body walking toward her. Her every instinct screamed at her to run, but she stayed in place. She began taking long, deep breaths and exhaling slowly, continuing her efforts to control herself.

It stopped a few feet in front of her. Self is designate 5309. Current location: within the neurochemical matrix of Kaia Little's biological unit.

"We're talking in my brain?!"

Correct.

"If that wasn't so completely messed up, this would be the coolest moment of my life. Are you… are you an alien?"

My limited understanding of Kaia's language center suggests that is an accurate description of self. Perhaps if Kaia Little were to download 5309's language center into her own, she would comprehend?

Her face registered shock. "You want to download your memories into my brain?" Kaia scratched her head. "Will it hurt?"

Insufficient data.

"No guts, no glory. Why shouldn't this day get weirder? Do it." 5309's form faded and suddenly Kaia felt an electrical jolt run through her body. She collapsed to the "ground" as millions of images flooded her brain. As the data stream filled her memory centers, she began twitching uncontrollably and her teeth began to chatter.

Then, to 5309's shock, she stopped moving at all.

Chapter 7
ARRIVAL PLUS 10 MINUTES: BONDING

The relentless torrent of memories finally stopped, and as it did, 5309 re-formed next to Kaia. This avatar of her consciousness had ceased functioning during the transfer, and he suddenly began to feel a swell of terror. In his life, he had never been one devoted to violence; if it were otherwise, he would have fought the Togai instead of running. But now, he was faced with the idea that he may have killed the first person he met on this new world.

Perhaps he deserved oblivion after all.

He scanned her biological unit again and detected that its functions seemed to be strengthening. Feeling a sense of relief, he chose to wait, his understanding of all that was happening tenuous at best. After a short passing of time, Kaia finally stirred.

"Oww. My head…"

5309… self… apologizes. Self…"

"I. Use the word 'I'. It's how individuals here refer to themselves. Occasionally a bit too much, but anyway… use 'I'."

Acknowledged. I apologize. I was unaware of how difficult the experience of sharing my memories with you would be.

"Apology accepted, especially after what I saw. Your planet… the society you came from… is kinda harsh. I can't even imagine it. An entire planet of bullies. I mean, I thought my life pretty much sucked, but yours takes the win."

I had no choice but to flee.

"True story, dude. Those Togai jerks meant serious business. The good news is, you landed somewhere cool, and you'll have friends here."

Friends? There was a pause. Yes, I would like

that very much.

"Any reason why I'm not fully awake yet, by the way?"

5309 formed fully in front of Kaia. There is something you need to know. When I arrived and collided with you… She felt a twinge of worry in her gut. Not understanding anything, my body went into shock and probed for a power source to reactivate itself. That power source was you, Kaia Little.

"Umm… what?"

We are bonded. My form is linked to your neurochemical system and is still drawing a slight bit of energy from it.

Kaia shivered. "Wait a minute… you're using my body's chemical systems and… converting to electrical power for your own body? That's messed up!"

In turn, I am regulating your biological unit's other systems.

"Still kinda terrifying and rude!"

I have healed fractures and lacerations caused by my arrival. My body is enveloped around yours…

"And it just got creepy. You're a boy, right?"

Gender is non-existent on Katahdin Prime. Is that the gender you prefer I identify as?

She rubbed her temples. "Oh, man. This day… Okay, look. I need to wake up soon. Danny is out there, and he is probably losing his mind."

I see no evidence of his brain having escaped his biological unit.

"Anyway… Look, this is too much right now. Let's work on the basics. First, you're going to need a name, not a number. Our world uses numbers for other things."

Your reasoning appears sound. Would you care to select one for me?

"Hmm. Well, you're all dark and spooky looking with the whole black motif, just like the Goth kids at my school. And considering they don't pick on me – not to mention gender questionable – I think we'll go with the obvious."

Danny continued caressing Kaia's hand, though he was uncertain if she could feel anything. The ebony substance surrounding her body continued to flow and move, but he was certain he could see her breathing within. "C'mon, Little, come back to me! I don't know what to do! I can't even call for help – the blast killed my cell phone." He gripped her arm tight. "And you have the stupid truck keys in your pocket!"

He let go and sat back on the ground. "I'm sorry, Kaia. I don't know what to do. I don't know."

Suddenly, Kaia's body began to move. The darkness surrounding her began shifting and reforming around her, draining away from her head, leaving it uncovered. She began coughing, and bits of black spittle escaped her lips. Danny stood up, watching intently as Kaia struggled to her feet.

A tear slid down Danny's cheek. "Umm, hi. You aren't dead." He bowed his head. "You're okay."

Kaia gave him a mysterious smile. "Dude, you don't know the half of it." She cocked her head. "Nice to know I'm worth crying over, though."

"Shut up. I was crying because you have the keys."

"Whatever. Wuss." She laughed, and he joined in after a moment. "So you're probably wondering about what I'm wearing."

Danny shrugged and wiped away a tear. "I'm sure lots of teenage girls have black bodysuits appear out of thin air. Not sure why you think you're special."

"Touché."

She closed her eyes for a moment, and as she opened them, the suit moved and flexed across her torso. When it stopped, two bright yellow eyes and a mouth appeared near her right collarbone.

"Danny, I'd like you to meet my new friend. His name is G'oth."

Chapter 8
ARRIVAL PLUS 15 MINUTES:
UNINVITED GUESTS

Major Stewart wiped sweat from his brow as the three scientists left in the building with him continued their attempts to regain control of the dish. He looked at their nametags for a moment, something he rarely did; nearing the end of his career, "the less I get attached, the better" was his thinking when he arrived at the S.E.T.I. project. Now, however, in the middle of a full-blown crisis, he adjusted his tactics. If things were to be salvaged, it would be because of these three young scientists.

"Dietrich, Frost, Drake," he repeated in his head.

"Mr. Drake, talk to me. I see we're still showing power spikes. I thought the power shutdown sequence was complete?"

The nervous young man clasped his hands on top of his bald head and stared at his computer screen. "We did, Major! I don't understand it. The dish should be dead in the water."

"But we're still broadcasting and locked," Frost said, interrupting his friend. "In fact," he started, then stopped for a moment to trace his index figure across a nearby screen, "the dish appears to be drawing more power than it should be able to."

Drake stood up. "That's crazy! We're reaching a point where we don't even have that kind of power to give it!"

Stewart began pacing. "It's damned odd. We've got to –"

Dietrich coolly pushed his chair away from his desk. "We've got to stop beating around the bush and admit to what's happening is what we've got to do."

"Mr. Dietrich?" Stewart said. "You have my attention."

The rest watched as Dietrich stood and began pacing. "The way this thing works is by opening a hole on the other end of the universe and shoving a signal through it. The universe is huge, vast, infinite… by lottery-sized odds, the hole should have opened up in the middle of nowhere."

"But?"

Dietrich shrugged. "Every bit of evidence we have at our disposal right now points to the exact opposite. We hit something. Something that has grabbed onto the dish's signal and is sending it power." He looked at Frost and Drake. "You two know it, too. You just didn't want to be the one to have to tell him," he said, pointing at Stewart.

The Major stood, rigid, his hands behind his back. He appraised the faces of the men in front of him carefully. The three scientists were doing their best to avoid looking Stewart in the eye, and the older man began to get aggravated. After a moment, though, he remembered that they were just civilians, and civilians who were likely terrified by what was happening. Breaking the silence, Stewart spoke in a quiet voice. "Do you all agree that this is what is happening?" Three heads nodded slowly in unison. "Very well. We find ourselves in quite a situation. I need options, people. Be creative."

Drake hopped out of his chair. "Break the machinery. Make it impossible for whoever is on the other end to use the dish."

Dietrich shook his head. "If whoever is on the other end has stabilized the tunnel, the dish could be irrelevant."

"Jam it," Frost chimed in.

"Go on," Stewart said.

"This is a radio dish at its heart. We sent a frequency across space. That frequency has locked onto something. We jam the signal with another one, broadcast something that disrupts that tunnel, and it stops."

A series of nods traveled the room. "Very well, Mr. Frost. Can you make that happen?"

"Yes, sir. With these guys' help, I think we can–"

Without warning, a disc of white energy appeared within the room, hovering a few feet over the four men's heads. The three scientists backed away, stumbling and falling to the ground, but Stewart stood unflinchingly, staring at this strange bit of lightning that had entered his command center.

The Major reached to his waist and reached for his holster. He felt for the handle of his sidearm, flexing his fingers. "You three move for the door. Anything happens and I will cover your exit. Whatever you do, get that jammer– "ZZZZZZZRRRRRRRKKKKKKKKKKK!

Chapter 9
ARRIVAL PLUS 20 MINUTES: TALES OF WHOA

Kaia folded her arms across her chest. "You just gonna sit there slack-jawed, dude? Gotta say, I expected better."

Danny cocked an eyebrow and stuck his tongue out at her. "Geez, what do you want me to say? An alien landed on Earth and bonded itself to you permanently." He began twirling his finger around. "Yay."

G'oth's face shifted to Kaia's arm, and the alien smiled. "It is wonderful that you are happy for your–"

"He's being sarcastic, G'oth. It's when… you know what, tap my memories and you'll get it." Kaia locked eyes with Danny. "Please tell me you're not gonna be a jerkweed about this." She exhaled. "Look, as much as I hate to say it, I need you on this."

"Six feet to the right." Danny said, his voice barely above a whisper.

"Six feet what?" Kaia replied.

The young boy ran his fingers through his hair. "Six feet to the right and he lands on me. An alien with the cool power to not only bond to a human, but fix every defect in their body."

"Oh, crap."

"So I just need a minute, okay? This is the coolest thing that will likely ever happen in either of our lifetimes, and I'm gonna get there, but right now, I'm hating on the universe a little bit."

"Understood." Kaia stepped away to give him space. Suddenly, she snapped her fingers. "G'oth! You fixed me – can you fix Danny?"

The alien's features moved to right above Kaia's heart. "Negative. Repairs are done at molecular level. I would have to bond with the boy as I have bonded with you."

"Can you do that?" she asked.

"If Kaia Little's life functions are fully terminated, and I survive the trauma, I could conceivably bond with another."

Kaia gave Danny a wan smile. "See, if I die, you're all set. And you thought you'd only get my laptop."

"You're very generous," Danny replied, smirking at her. "Alright, moving on." He walked over and placed his hand against Kaia's back, feeling the energy pulsing through G'oth. "Have you thought about what you can do? Together, I mean?"

"Explain," G'oth said.

"You mentioned that you learned to shape-shift back home. Can you do that while attached to Kaia?"

She tilted her head, looking skeptical of what Danny was saying. "Where is this going?'

Danny began pacing. "You say he can tap your memories, but he can also tap your conscious memory as well. That was what he was doing while you were out. So what I'm saying is: think of something, and see if he can shift into it."

"Such as?"

"Start basic. Think comics. Or anime. Yeah! Like some killer mecha stuff!"

With a nod, Kaia closed her eyes for a moment. As they snapped open, G'oth began to rapidly change shape around her. Where she had once been covered in a smooth bodysuit, Kaia was now wearing a suit of what looked like high-tech armor. Metallic-looking boots, thick legs, a full torso, huge arms, and a rounded helmet with openings for the eyes and mouth now covered her body. G'oth's own features served as a "belt-buckle" across her midsection, and a symbol that resembled a human standing in a maze appeared on her chest.

"Whaddaya think?" she asked.

Danny walked around her in a slow circle. "Not bad. The journey symbol is a nice touch."

"Wow. You actually do pay attention to me."

"Here's question number two: how tough is G'oth compared to our world? This looks like armor, but what happens if you actually hit it with something?"

"I don't think that's –" Before she could finish

her sentence, Danny reached down to the ground, grabbed a thick tree branch, and hit her as hard as he could across her shoulder blades. At impact, the branch exploded into dozens of pieces, the splinters spreading through the air and littering the ground.

As the chunks of wood were still in the air, Kaia/G'oth spun around faster than Danny would have believed possible. During that split second, a series of laser gun turrets formed out of her right arm, each one glowing with energy… and now pointed at Danny's head.

"Hey!" Danny screamed. "Stop!" For a long second, the turrets remained aimed at him, then she stood down, Danny sighing in relief. "Okay, so I think we've determined that you have defense mechanisms and weaponry as part of the deal," Danny said, shaken.

The helmet melted away. "Sorry. Sorry. I don't know what happened there. Sorry. Sorry."

Danny backed away a couple of steps. "Nah, it's… it's probably a cool thing. Might as well run with what we've got. Try firing the guns."

She shook her head. "No way. That's not a good idea."

"You kidding? We're on the edge of nowhere right now. I'll bet thousands of kids have learned to shoot a weapon out near these rocks and trees. You've got it, so use it."

"G'oth?"

"Ready." He shifted his body and recreated the helmet. Kaia raised her arm and signaled for the gun turrets. They formed around her arm and she took aim at a large boulder about thirty feet away. There was a brief delay as Kaia reconsidered, then a jolt of adrenalin as she willed the guns to fire.

A red energy bolt ripped through the air and struck the rock four feet off the ground. There was a loud explosion and a burst of flame, smoke filling the air. They watched as sparks flickered into the night, then stood in awe as the boulder, now completely severed in two, fell backward and thudded to the ground with a resounding thud.

"Whoa," Danny said, his eyes wide.

"Whoa, indeed," Kaia said, nodding slowly. "Whoa, indeed."

Chapter 10
ARRIVAL PLUS 25 MINUTES:
THE ENEMY WITHOUT

"LET. ME. OUT!" Stewart struck out at the darkness that surrounded him. There was no light, no indication of depth, nothing... he was lost, and his every instinct told him he had been imprisoned. "Who are you? Why are you doing this? We mean no harm!"

A deep echoing voice penetrated the blackness. "I am 84A of the Togai. Your biological unit has been commandeered as part of pursuit of fugitive. Your species has interfered in the affairs of Katahdin

Prime by facilitating an escape. This will not stand."

The older man growled. "So you've taken over my body without asking? Sounds like maybe we did a good thing by helping your prisoner escape. I get the feeling you aren't the good guys. Togai, I think you called yourself?"

"Your thoughts and feelings are irrelevant. Your species is irrelevant. Only the mission matters."

Stewart felt his anger rising, then took steps to calm himself. "First, assess the threat," he reminded himself.

"Irrelevant," came 84A's voice from the dark.

"Go smell a shoe," Stewart said, diving deeper into his head. He focused on his inner core, and as he did, an idea began to form in his mind.

84A spoke again, sounding weary. "Your efforts are futile."

"Then go do what you're here to do and stop bothering me," Stewart snapped. There was a long pause, and the older man suddenly sensed that the alien had turned its attention elsewhere. "Huh. Okay," he thought. "Time to put years of military discipline to work," he thought, sitting down in a cross-legged position. As he did, he closed his eyes and began to focus inward again, he slowed down his breathing.

Then, in a moment that made the older man smile, a mental brick formed in front of him on the ground. Certain he was on the right path, he redoubled his efforts, and more bricks began to appear. No way was this alien going to keep free access to his brain. Not now. Not ever.

84C heard the sound first, an explosion in the distance. He analyzed it quickly, determining that it had to have come from the quadrant he was assigned to search for the fugitive. He checked his bearings and saw small flickers of light in an area to his northwest. Intrigued, he changed direction to check it out.

Sadly, the creature named Drake, whose body he had usurped, was of no use. Its adrenal glands had overloaded and the conscious and subconscious mind had shut down due to terror. What glimpses and knowledge he had been able to glean were mostly about the facility where the Togai had landed and about the creature's efforts to try and shut down the tunneling effect to Katahdin Prime.

Moving stealthily through the desert grasses and weeds between the facility and the flickering lights, 84C began to hear the sound of voices. He slowed his approach, taking caution – the locals were an unknown variable as of yet – but once he got within visual range, he saw something that truly shocked him: the fugitive had bonded with one of the locals, and was clearly working with another local to plot weapons strategy.

Following proper procedure, 84C sent a signal to the others that he had located the fugitive and was about to engage. Taking his sword in his hand, he began to feel the energy surge through it, charging it to maximum power. Once it reached critical levels, he raised it and aimed at the fugitive.

"Gun turrets, full-on cannon, sword… your alien pal is pretty handy, Kaia." Danny watched a small fire burn out. "I suspect we… you… could get even more creative with the shapes around your body, too." His eyes glazed for a moment. "I bet you could even be a giant."

"A weak one," she countered. "It's not like I'm adding mass. Do you ever pay attention in physics?"

Danny shrugged. "That's why I pay you to tutor me."

Before Kaia could reply, a massive bolt of energy struck her in the back and sent her flying. She crashed into a nearby tree, breaking it in two and toppling it, and she landed face-first on the ground, steam rising from her body.

"Kaia!" Danny started to run, but as he took his third step, a creature emerged from the darkness. It reminded him immediately of G'oth, but this one was brown. In its right hand was a sword that glowed a bright red, and the creature brought the sword up and pointed it at him.

"Unknown biological unit: collaboration with escaped prisoner marks you as a criminal. According to Katahdin Prime law, you are hereby sentenced to—"

In a moment of déjà vu, Danny stood wide-eyed as a blast of energy struck the Togai warrior and sent it flying into the nearby grasses. The young boy shook his head, startling himself back to full awareness, and turned his attention to Kaia.

No longer face-down on the ground, she was fully armored within G'oth and walking with purpose toward the Togai warrior. "OWWW. That hurt! Shoot me in the back, jerkweed?" The gun turrets formed at the end of her arm. "Not. Cool."

"Not cool at all."

Chapter 11
ARRIVAL PLUS 30 MINUTES: SHOWTIME

G'oth's voice echoed loudly in her head: RUN!

Kaia asserted herself within the bond. "No! All I ever do is turn the other cheek and walk away. I'm sick of bullies! You should be, too!"

The Togai will not stop until my life functions are at an end. We must flee!

"No. I'm tired of running! We can beat this guy."

Where there is one, there are three others.

"First things first." She shifted G'oth until she was once again holding a sword that matched the one the Togai was carrying.

"Danny, take cover!" Kaia yelled at him from behind the helmet. The young boy dove beneath the truck and watched as she approached the brown alien. "You need time to recharge, dude," Kaia said, her voice filled with swagger. "So let's do this the old-fashioned way."

She raised the sword and charged at her Togai opponent, causing him to do the same. As they passed one another, the swords collided, setting off a wave of sparks and sending a loud hissing sound through the air. In unison, both turned around and ran at each other again, once again resulting in a blinding splash of sparks.

Kaia turned around slowly, taking in the sight of her Togai opponent. It raised its sword again and swung in her direction, but she nimbly sidestepped the strike. Again, the Togai reared back with all of its might and swung down on her, but she quickly moved aside.

The Togai made a noise of frustration.

"G'oth, I have a confession to make," Kaia said, her voice slightly quivering.

This sounds as though it is troubling.

"The only experience with sword fighting I have is in playing video games. This was probably kind of stupid on my part."

This is most definitely troubling.

Danny watched in awe as Kaia/G'oth dodged blow after blow from the Togai warrior. As they did, Danny could see that the Togai's sword was charging quite slowly. "It must lose energy every time he hits something – even if it's the ground," he thought. "Hope they can take advantage of that."

It was a ballet of violence like he had never seen. Countless hours of video games and Hollywood movies had not prepared him for what combat between two alien species would actually look like.

We cannot defeat him with this weapon. We must run!

"Yeah, I know, I'm sorry. Stupid on my part. Stupid. I – wait a minute! That's it!"

What is 'it'?

"Find me a weak spot. And be ready."

The Togai swung down on Kaia/G'oth again, and this time, they parried the strike with their own sword. Rather than backing away, though, the Togai pressed down with all its might, trying to press an advantage.

"Submit, criminal, to the justice of Katahdin Prime! Accept your punishment!" 84C spoke with a sneer in his voice. "You merely compound your crimes by bonding with this lesser."

The faceplate on the helmet slid away, displaying most of Kaia's face. "Lesser? I can get that in the girls' bathroom in my school. Got any other names you want to call me?"

84C formed a frown on his face. "You are clearly a member of an inferior species, compounded by your bond with this –

"ZZZZAAAAAAARRRRK!!!!!!!!!!!!!!!!!

The Togai looked down to see its body melting away, dripping away from its host. Pointed at his torso was a series of gun turrets extending from the fugitive's other arm, the turrets smoking with energy. In that moment, he knew he had failed as completely as any Togai in the history of his species.

"Lesser," Kaia continued, "but still a better lateral thinker."

She watched as the alien warrior dropped to the ground and melted away from a human male's body. He was wearing a nametag that said 'Drake' and from his clothing, she thought he had to have been a scientist for the dish. She felt around until she detected a weak pulse.

"He's alive!"

Yes. He has been freed from involuntarily serving the Togai.

Kaia's thoughts swirled for a moment. "G'oth… I…"

You need not be troubled. Your actions did not end the life of another. The Togai's central system will broadcast its knowledge and experience back to its crèche. At the end of a generation, the crèche will recreate the Togai as a new generation, complete with all memories from before.

"So they're kinda immortal?"

If I understand your meaning, yes.

"Doesn't that mean they can send massive reinforcements as soon as that guy gets back?"

The Togai's recreate over a span of time matching five of your planet's days. His knowledge will remain unknown to others until then.

"I don't want to kill anyone," she said, attempting to gather herself.

The remaining Togai will not show us the same kindness.

Danny got out from under the truck and knelt next to the scientist. "What do we do now?"

Kaia snapped out of her reveries and began pacing. "They come in packs of four, these Togai warriors. If he alerted them he'd seen us, they'll be on their way."

"Uh oh."

A large hole developed in the right side of the armor. Kaia reached in and pulled out the keys to the truck. "Get this guy back to the dish. See if there's any way of contacting help when you get there."

"And you?"

She stifled a yawn. "First, I need every energy drink we have in the cooler. Being a human battery is kinda tiring and I need electrolytes." Danny climbed into the back and began pulling bottles out of the cooler. "Then I'm going to go after the Togai and try and stop them."

"That's the dumbest thing I've ever heard. And I've been here all night."

Kaia opened a bottle and began guzzling. "I have to keep them away from the dish and away from you." Sensing Danny's displeasure, she continued, "So until you come up with a better plan, this is what we're stuck with."

Chapter 12
ARRIVAL PLUS 35 MINUTES:
THE ENEMY PLOTS

84A felt it first, a disruptive wave of energy passing through his body. Within that wave of energy, he could smell the scent of fear and disgust that had emanated from his comrade as he faded away on this misbegotten world where they had landed. Activating a carrier wave between himself and the other two, he announced what they all knew: "84C is no longer vital and active. His failure will attach itself to each of us if we do not finish this mission successfully.

"Understood," came the replies from 84B and 84D.

"It was clear from his last transmission that he was about to engage the fugitive. We must assume that the criminal acquired ordinance on this world that allowed him to defeat one of us. This cannot stand." Again, the other two Togai offered assent. "We will change our course of action. Both of you, make haste for the quadrant where 84C was last known to be. Together, we represent far more force than the fugitive can possibly withstand."

84B and D acknowledged the order, and each altered their course, heading for the rocks, desert weeds, and trees at the far field from the dish. Communication ceased as each one moved at their best possible speed toward where 84C had fallen. 84B was closest, and in the distance, his ocular sensors detected movement. This caused him to stop to examine what he was seeing.

"Request for hold," 84B said. "I have movement ahead and am working through tactical responses."

"Granted," 84A replied. "Your observations?"

There was a flat tone to 84B's voice. "A

conveyance of some sort. It is moving in a direction that would suggest it is traveling back to the area where we made our arrival."

Silence set in between the Togai as 84A pondered what to do. "Troubling scenarios. If the conveyance contains the fugitive, which would be logical, he may be attempting to return to Katahdin Prime."

"With a weapon that can harm Togai."

84A continued. "An unacceptable outcome. The fugitive must be dealt with here, on this primitive world."

"Not as primitive as we would like," 84D sneered.

"Your impertinence is noted," 84A said, his voice raising only slightly, "and your statement contains truth. We must cover all aspects of this incident to be certain that this criminal does not continue to roam free."

In his peripheral vision, 84A could see the conveyance moving in the distance. Its motion indicated a solid, but not spectacular speed, and it was indeed heading toward the location where the Togai had arrived. "The conveyance is now within my field of vision. Tactical adjustment: 84B, proceed to last known area where 84C was known to be, examine any evidence that indicates how the fugitive accomplished his dissolution."

"It will be done."

"84D, you will make best speed toward our arrival point, as will I. We will confront and destroy the fugitive, as well as secure the portal that will return us to Katahdin Prime. The less time we spend on this world, the better." 84A turned his thoughts inward again and discovered that he could no longer see Stewart; instead, the older man was encased behind a series of brick walls he had created within his consciousness to block 84A out. "Advise you keep an eye on your biological unit host; no disruptions."

With that, the link between the Togai went quiet.

As he moved through the tall desert grasses, 84B turned his gaze inward. The creature known as Dietrich was still quiet and unaware of 84B's presence. The shock of the Togai's arrival, as well as the bonding process, had rendered this Dietrich inert. "Surely," he thought, "all of this planet's denizens would respond in that fashion? Who would not immediately be overcome by the power and majesty of a warrior of Katahdin Prime?"

Noticing a dimming light ahead, 84B began charging his sword. Only a few seconds later, he exited the grasses and found something he had never seen: a Togai in a state of dissolution. Were it within his biological imperatives, he would have felt a wave of nausea and responded with immediate illness; however, all he felt instead was a wave of anger, followed by sadness. "The dimming of your light darkens us all," 84B said, a solemn tone in his voice.

KRRRRRREAK

The Togai spun around and raised his sword. Standing in front of him, only a few yards away, was one of the local biological units. It was smaller, and on the surface, it had a number of external characteristics that were different that those the Togai had bonded with. It was wearing clothing of simple fibers, and items that he assumed were adornments. "Stand your ground, biological unit.

Do not interfere in the affairs of the Togai."

The small creature's orifices seemed to tremble. "Please, help," it said. "My friend… he needs help."

84B waived her away. "I have no time for this. Dismiss yourself from this locale immediately."

"My friend gave me this bracelet," it said, holding up its arm. "Now I need to help him."

"It is no concern of mine," the Togai said in disgust. "Away with you."

To his surprise, the creature gave him a small look of pleasure. "Well that's just rude of you. I don't like rude people." The Togai's eyes widened as the bracelet began to move and flow around the creature. "My name's Kaia, by the way." She was now clad in full armor.

"I believe you already know my friend."

Chapter 13
ARRIVAL PLUS 40 MINUTES: AWAKENING

Out of the corner of his eye, Danny could see Drake returning to consciousness. "Dude? Sir? Can you hear me?"

The scientist groaned and shifted his body in the seat, slightly flailing his arms. Then he reached with both hands and began feeling his face. "Huh? Wuzzat? Izzat me?"

"Look, man, I'll throw this at you quickly: yes, it's you. No, you're not possessed by an alien anymore. Yes, you're in a moving vehicle. Does that cover it?

Because it's been a bit of a rough evening, and we desperately need you to pull it together, okay?"

Drake's eyes fluttered open. "Wow. That was pretty cranky, kid."

Danny turned to face him. "I'll be nicer if we can stop the alien invasion. How's that?"

"Well, by all means," Drake said with a derisive snort. "I assume you have a plan?"

"Was kind of hoping you did."

Laughter echoed through the truck. "Then it's your lucky night kid, because me and my buddies do."

"They're still kinda occupied by alien possession right now," Danny said, his voice dropping.

Drake looked out the windshield at the dish. "Then I guess you and I are gonna save the world, kid."

Kaia landed a punch square in the middle of 84B's head, sending the Togai staggering backward. Sensing an opening, she swung again, catching the alien in the shoulder this time, causing it to spin away from her. As it did, 84B focused what energies he had into his sword and swung it around. The flat side caught Kaia in the ribs and sent her sprawling across the ground.

I am unaware of what this strategy is meant to accomplish.

"You've been on my planet less than an hour and you already understand sarcasm," Kaia thought back.

May I once again suggest running?

"NO!" she screamed in her thoughts, the sound vibrating her skull. "I'm so so so tired of running. Every day. Every day I turn the other cheek. I take it and take it and take it, and every day I feel smaller. I'm tired of being 'less', G'oth. With you, I have the power to stand, and that's what I'm going to – "

WHOOOOOOMMMMMMMM

Kaia rolled out of the way just in time, as 84B jammed his sword into the ground where her head had been. Picking herself up off the ground, she formed the gun turret around her wrist. "That all you got?" she asked 84B. Taking aim, she fired at him with every barrel.

Unfortunately, 84B was ready. He raised his

sword and the blast hit it with maximum impact. But rather than be injured or knocked down, the sword absorbed all of the energy Kaia and G'oth had emitted. Glowing dark red, and nearly faster than they could react, 84B returned fire, hitting Kaia and G'oth in the left hip. Kaia let out a blood-curdling scream that shattered the night air and fell to the ground in pain. In her head, G'oth whimpered in deep pain.

With a smooth, deliberate stride, 84B made his way to Kaia's prone form. "Your criminal ways are at an end, fugitive. You fought well, I grant you, but your fight is now over."

We are doomed! G'oth's voice was filled with terror. I am so sorry Kaia Little. Your lifespan was meant to be longer, of that I am certain.

Struggling to gain her voice and push the pain aside, Kaia focused on G'oth's presence. "No… we aren't finished yet. We can't be."

I am at a loss for potential actions.

She searched her memory for a moment, and suddenly it came to her. "Wait – you said you learned to change your shape back home. I'm guessing you can do a lot more than this armor and the weaponry."

Yes, but...

"Follow my lead."

84B began the process of charging his sword, energies pulsing and flowing through it. As it did, he aimed it at the center of Kaia/G'oth's chest. Suddenly, the visor on the helmet opened, exposing the face of the local lifeform.

"You think you've won, don't you?" its tone conveying disgust.

The tip of the sword rested on the fugitive's body. "It is over. Accept your fate and punishment. Resistance is futile at this juncture." As 84B spoke, he focused on Kaia's eyes. Doing so meant he missed the thin sliver of G'oth that slithered away from his body, moving along the ground until it was behind the Togai.

"Resistance is life. And I'm not alone out here," the lifeform said defiantly. "My friend has me covered."

The tendril of G'oth began rising behind 84B,

unbeknownst to the alien hunter. "There are no other lifeforms in this vicinity. And now – "

"Really? What about him?" the lifeform asked. At the same time, he felt a strong tapping on his shoulder. 84B spun around quickly, seeing only empty space behind him. Momentarily confused, he stopped for a moment, then turned back to Kaia/ G'oth.

ZZZZAAAAAAARRRRRRK!!!!!!!!!!!!!!

The blast from the gun turrets shocked 84B's system to the core, and he let out a stifled cry of shock. Standing tall in front of him, and watching as he sank to the ground and began experiencing dissolution, was the fugitive and the local lifeform it had bonded with. The lifeform's expression was one of satisfaction and surprise.

As the Togai vanished, Kaia watched as the body of a man named Frost was revealed.

"Two down," she whispered to herself. "But why aren't the others here? They should have all come for us." After a moment of thought, she understood the answer. "Oh, no. Nonononono."

Chapter 14
ARRIVAL PLUS 45 MINUTES:
TALK OF SACRIFICE

Danny and Drake entered the dish's control room. Drake immediately sat as his station and began checking readouts, then started sliding his chair around to look at his friends' computers.

"Looks like the Togai arriving didn't do too much damage," Danny said, scanning the room.

"Not to the equipment," Drake said with a bitter tone. Standing up, he looked out of the nearest window. "Looks like the tunnel is now directly over the dish."

"I thought you said it was stable?"

Drake snorted. "It is. But as the Earth moves through space, it's giving slight shifts and bends to the tunnel…"

"…dragging it. I get it."

The scientist stood and walked across the room, stopping in front of an electrical panel. He ran his fingers along the edge, then gripped hard and pulled it open. Inside were dozens of wires and cables, and without stopping, Drake began pulling them out and into the open.

"Hey kid: what do you know about frequencies and sound?" Drake asked.

Danny stopped himself from laughing. "More than you might think. Why?"

"Because that's what we need to do. The tunnel is stabilized on a particular frequency. So if we can broadcast a jamming frequency through it, the whole thing should implode and seal itself."

"Sounds easy enough," Danny replied.

Drake rolled his eyes. "Sure. Except for a few problems. The energy released from the collapse could blow up the entire installation. Including us."

"That seems problematic."

"Yeah. Also, the energy in play out there is vibrating the dish to the point where the supersonic sounds must be driving dogs crazy for a fifty mile radius. Going out there… well, no human's hearing can survive that, and that's assuming it didn't fry your entire nervous system first. Which it probably would."

Danny tapped him on the shoulder to make sure he was looking at him. Sure that Drake was paying attention, he reached up and plucked his hearing aid from his one good ear. "LOOKS LIKE IT'S YOUR LUCKY DAY, MR. DRAKE."

84A felt a twinge of pain and shock. He reached out with his thoughts and located only 84D. "You have felt it?" he asked his remaining partner.

"I have," came the reply.

"Our quarry was still in the vicinity of where 84C reached dissolution, not at our current destination. We were deceived."

84D could not mask his displeasure. "You were deceived. You are at fault for the incompetent loss of our brethren. Your fitness for the position of 'A' must be called into question."

Anger rose within the lead Togai. "You dare question me? Were we not in the midst of a mission, I would administer punishment upon you, without mercy."

"Or perhaps I would take the mantle of 'A' from you."

"This line of discussion is pointless! Focus on the quarry! We have a task to complete. A new stratagem is required."

"What would you have us do now? Reverse course and move toward where the other two of us fell?"

The line of communication went quiet for a moment as 84A thought out the permutations for potential actions. "No. We continue along this path and enter the structure. If the quarry was not in the conveyance, someone else was. That gives us the upper hand and forces the quarry to come to us…"

"…Because we have leverage in the form of hostages." 84D brightened. "An excellent plan."

"Of this, I am aware," 84A said without a trace

of emotion.

Kaia/G'oth ran through the desert scrub at a blistering pace; looking at the movement of objects as they went past, she estimated they were going at least 60 miles per hour. "And this is among the least weird things about my night," she laughed to herself.

It was G'oth who had the stratagem this time. If you are willing and able to allow me to control your body, I can get us there far more quickly than you can.

"How?" she had wondered.

Go limp.

As she did so, her legs began pumping and running. This was a new sensation; G'oth was in full control over her, physically, and she wondered if this was what it felt like for the guys who had been taken over by the Togai. She pushed that thought away, though, knowing that if she was going to save Danny – not to mention anyone else nearby – letting G'oth do his thing was the right move.

By forming a "seat" that held Frost in place on

her back, they were also able to carry the groggy and not yet alert scientist with them. Thanks to G'oth being in control, she did not feel the extra weight, and they were making good time as they raced back to the dish.

The lighting from the installation began gaining in intensity as they approached. Then, and only then, did Kaia give in to all of the horrible things in her mind: "Is Danny still alive?" "Is there a way to shut down the tunnel to Katahdin Prime?" "Do I have even the slightest of chances to beat two Togai, when I can barely beat one?"

"Is Danny still alive?"

Chapter 15
ARRIVAL PLUS 50 MINUTES:
HERE COMES THE BOOM

"Hand me that screwdriver, kid," Drake said, holding out his right hand. In his left was a foot-long cylinder of wires and tech that Danny didn't even remotely understand. The young boy placed the screwdriver gently into the scientist's open palm and watched as the older man tightened what looked like a small matchbox to the outside of the cylinder.

"I wonder if I told my teacher about this, I could get extra credit in science class," Danny said.

Drake barked a quick laugh. "Helping stop an

alien invasion out to get you a few points at least. Of course, if your teacher asks you to explain it…"

"Blah blah harmonics, blah blah, quantum tunneling effect, blah blah kaboom." Danny shrugged his shoulders. "Okay, so it might be an issue if she asks me to write a paper about it."

"Tough luck." Drake focused in on finishing what he was doing, while Danny absently looked around the room. The boy realized that he could feel the vibrations from the dish and from the tunnel. There was a subtle hum permeating the room, and when he touched the wall, he could feel it ebb through his body.

After a minute of silence passed, Danny began wrinkling his nose. "Huh. That's weird."

Without looking up, Drake said "What's weird? Besides this entire night, if course."

"I'd swear I smell burning metal. You don't smell it?"

This time, Drake looked up. He began sniffing at the air and nodding his head. "I think you may be right. I wonder if – "

KRAAAAKATABOOOOOOOOOOM

The wall behind them exploded inward, sending shrapnel across the room, cutting Danny and Drake in many places. Smoke wafted and curled through the hole, and Drake quickly dropped the jamming device to the floor and hid it behind him. When the smoke finally cleared, they watched the remaining two Togai glide into the room.

"Lifeforms: you are now prisoners of the Togai. Your existence will be used as leverage to draw out a fugitive who has escaped justice. If you provide us with no reason to harm you, we may select that option. Should you choose to resist, we will deliver you punishment." Danny thought he saw the creature snarl. "You will not enjoy it."

Drake swallowed and gathered his courage. "You have no authority here," he said, a slight quiver in his voice. "This is not your world, this is Earth, and we do not recognize your law or your power. Leave now, and we will… well, we'll just let this whole thing go. Otherwise, we'll be forced to retaliate."

The Togai turned to face one another, obviously communicating amongst themselves. Watching, Danny whispered out of the side of his mouth. "That was some grade-A crap you were talking. Think it will work?"

"If it does, I'm leaving here tonight and immediately buying a lotto ticket," Drake whispered back.

Done communicating, the Togai shifted their attention back to their hostages. "The law of Katahdin Prime supersedes the laws of all other planets. You will draw the fugitive here, and he will be punished. Or we will start by punishing you, and then continue by making an example out of the rest of this primitive world you call 'Earth."

Danny felt a chill roll down his spine.

"You see it?" Kaia asked.

I do. I also heard it. The Togai just threatened your world with war against Katahdin Prime.

"We can't let that happen! We have to stop them, G'oth!"

What stratagem do you have in mind? We have only beaten the Togai so far with the aid of good fortune. There are two. Our chances of success are –

"I'd rather not know. And we don't have to beat

them. We just have to get them to chase us and get away from whatever the boys are going to do to shut that space doorway."

"War, then?" Drake spat in the direction of the Togai.

"It is your choice," 84A said.

KRAAAAKATABOOOOOOOOOOM

The ceiling above them exploded in fury, a massive chunk dropping to the ground between the humans and the Togai. As sparks, papers, and wiring rained down into the control room, a massive figure dropped through the hole and landed with a loud thud only a few feet in front of Danny and Drake.

"Hope you don't mind me dropping in uninvited," Kaia said. "But I was in the neighborhood." Astonished, Drake went mute, but Danny could not stop himself from smiling. "Mr. Drake," she said, pointing her thumb to her back and Frost, "I believe this belongs to you." The straps holding Frost to her back slowly dissolved, allowing Danny and Drake to catch the groggy scientist.

84A raised his sword, pointing it at Kaia/G'oth.

"Fugitive. You came as we knew you would. Surrender now and spare these lifeforms. Spare this world. Do not force me to share your punishment with them."

"You're nothing more than a bully," Kaia replied. "A cosmic bully, but a bully nonetheless." The gun turrets formed around her right wrist and the sword grew out of her left.

"I don't like bullies," she said, a quiet finality in her voice.

Chapter 16
ARRIVAL PLUS 55 MINUTES:
A MERRY CHASE

Kaia stretched her left arm quickly across the room and swiped at 84D with the sword. At the same time, she took aim at 84A and fired her energy blasts. The blast hit 84A directly in the torso, sending the Togai sprawling to the ground. However, 84D parried with his own sword, causing Kaia and G'oth to cry out in pain.

"OWWWWW!" She inhaled, trying to manage the hurt. "What was that?"

The farther I stretch my body, the weaker those

extensions become, remember?

"Got it. Don't extend you too far. Ouch!"

The arm and sword retracted back to Kaia's body as 84D followed with his sword raised high. "You will be destroyed, criminal, and I will take great pleasure in it!"

"Gotta catch me first," Kaia yelled. As she did, springs formed on the bottom of her feet and she began to bounce. Once, twice, and then she bounced high enough that she went right back through the hole in the ceiling. Simultaneously, 84D fired his sword and missed, blowing a hole in the wall behind Danny and the scientists.

Standing under the hole in the ceiling, 84D growled in anger, then jumped through the opening, disappearing from view.

"Frost! Hey, man, wake up!" Drake said, jostling his friend. "Need ya, dude."

With a shudder, Frost gathered himself. "Drake? I just had the strangest dream. I was – "

"That was no dream, man, it was your life. Get therapy later. Right now, we kinda gotta save the planet. These aliens aren't exactly the friendly type, and the doorway back to their place is still wide open."

"Aww, man... it is all true, isn't it? We were poss– "

"Therapy. Later. Jammer. Now." Drake said, his voice filled with rising urgency. He handed Frost the device he had been working on. "This is what I've got. Will it work?"

Frost took it in his hands and began looking it over. He studied it carefully for a moment, then shook his head. "Almost. But it needs a broader wavelength. This would have only annoyed and maybe extended the quantum effects. You have it set too tight. Got a screwdriver?" Danny handed the scientist the tool and watched as he fiddled around inside the device. A minute passed as he worked, until he finally snapped it shut. "There. That ought to do it. What's the plan?"

Danny cleared his throat. "I am," he said, taking his hearing aid out.

Kaia/G'oth landed in the employee parking lot.

"Hey! That worked great," she gushed. "I could get good at this!"

The springs were indeed clever. What other concepts do you have that may assist us in staying alive?

"Killjoy." She started thinking about the comics and cartoons she had watched over the years and what else she could borrow from them. "I'll come up with something."

Our time has become limited. Look!

84D moved like lightning across the roof and descended to the parking lot without breaking stride. "Let us end this," he bellowed. "No more running."

"If that's the way you want it," Kaia replied. She let out a loud growl of her own, then charged the Togai, tackling it around the midsection. "Bet you don't have football on your stupid, crappy planet, do ya?" She began to punch the Togai with all of their combined might, pummeling the alien in its midsection repeatedly.

"HRRRRGH!" 84D barked, trying to regain control. The fugitive was not truly damaging him, but it was disrupting his connection to the local lifeform he was bonded to. Focusing his thoughts inward, he concentrated on ignoring what was being done to him, and instead made an effort to raise his arms. As he did, he used the flat side of his sword and swatted the fugitive off of him, sending the criminal skidding across the ground and into a conveyance, nearly destroying it.

"That… super sucked…" Kaia said, feeling the pain in her back radiate throughout her body.

I believe I understand your meaning. And you are correct.

"Aww, man… he knocked us into a Corvette." She braced herself against what was left of the car and stood up. "Such a nice car. Sorry, owner dude." She looked up and saw 84D taking aim with a fully charged sword. With no time to shift to anything clever, she ripped the door off of what was left of the car and whipped it around in front of her, using it as a shield to block the blast, ultimately reducing the door to tiny pieces of scrap metal.

Angered, 84D raced at Kaia/G'oth, swinging his sword violently. The pair formed their sword, blocking some shots, dodging many others.

"Anybody ever tell you," Kaia said breathlessly, "that you have serious anger management issues?"

The Togai did not reply, keeping up its attacks. It was a dance of destruction, as their path took them past several cars, the Togai's sword slicing into many of them with wild abandon. "I mean it! You're crazy!" she yelled at him. In turn he struck down at her, sending her diving to the ground as the sword sliced through the engine block of a nearby van, sending pieces across the pavement. Kaia watched in astonishment as the Togai pulled his sword free and began righting himself.

Kaia's attention, however, was elsewhere.

"Do you see what I see?"

It is impossible not to. I am bonded to your ocular system.

"Not what I meant. You and I, we're a battery, right? The Togai have bonded to humans just like you did, right, so they are, too? Right?"

Essentially correct.

"So what happens when you run a disruptive current through a battery?"

Nothing good. Ahh, I believe I understand your thinking.

"Can you insulate us from it?"

I believe so, yes.

The Togai warrior saw them on the ground, motionless, and moved in for the kill. 84D felt a feeling of smug satisfaction, as 84A had obviously yet to recover and join the hunt. The victory was to be his and his alone. He would complete this mission. He would ascend to the A position in the next generation. It was a day to savor.

Kaia's visor flipped up and she stared at the Togai. "You win. We surrender to your judgment. Just spare me; it is him that you want."

"You must also be punished as an accomplice. There is no mercy for such as you, lifeform of Earth."

She smiled. "Too bad. I was just starting to like it here. I'm even getting an 'A' in science class." He raised his sword above her head to deliver the final blow, but as he did, he saw that the fugitive had wrapped a piece of itself around a small, rectangular object in the nearby wreckage. Before he could question or react, a second piece of the fugitive leapt forward and wrapped around his neck.

What came next was excruciatingly painful, as the current from the van's battery was delivered into the Togai's body in one burst, shattering its bond with Dietrich. As 84D melted away, G'oth retracted his body until their armored form was at maximum again.

"That felt... weird," Kaia said, watching her foe dissipate.

I wasn't able to fully insulate us.

"Let's not do it again." She looked in the direction of the dish and saw energy still coalescing above it. "Huh. They still haven't closed the tunnel."

We are also missing an opponent.

"That is so not good."

Chapter 17
ARRIVAL PLUS 60 MINUTES:
AN UNPLEASANT SURPRISE

Danny sat on his backside at the edge of the dish, watching sparks of lightning crackle back and forth across his field of vision. On the far side, he could see the white energy disc – the tunnel opening – floating about ten feet above. Deciding that lower was better, he flattened himself against the dish's surface and began crawling on his belly toward the other side.

It was not fast going.

A stray bolt arced across his back, causing his

hair to stand on end. When it was done, he felt his leg begin to twitch uncontrollably, causing him to wonder if it was from the electricity or from terror. He also began to ponder the ramifications of things going wrong, his paranoia slowing him down further.

"What if the jammer gets hit? What if I get hit? What if the jammer doesn't work? What is that digging into my leg?" He felt, and it was his hearing aid in his pocket. "Why didn't I make one of those scientists do this? I could use more deaf friends…"

Onward, he crawled, until he finally saw the far edge was only a few feet away. He looked up, and for reasons not immediately explainable, the tunnel seemed to be blotted out by a huge brown cloud.

"Huge brown cloud?" He paused and focused his vision. "Uh oh…"

Danny rolled onto his back and propped himself up on his elbows. Towering over him was 84A, standing between him and the tunnel opening.

"Your courage is almost admirable, tiny Earthling. With no weaponry, you have survived this long, and you have come so close to your goal."

Danny read the creature's lips perfectly. "But you will not be allowed to complete your mission. The doorway to Katahdin Prime will remain open until the fugitive has been dealt with." 84A reached toward him. "Give me the device, and I will allow your existence to continue."

The young boy sat slack-jawed for a moment, terrified of the being in front of him, and uncertain of what to do. Looking side-to-side, he could see that there was nowhere to run. There was nowhere to hide.

He had a choice to make.

"I don't want to die," he said, his voice quivering.

"Good…"

"But I can't let you hurt anyone else, either."

84A tilted his head in disgust. As he did, Danny saw a black tendril rise behind the Togai warrior's back. He watched in amazement as it began forming letters in American Sign Language (ASL): O-N-T-H-E-C-O-U-N-T-O-F-3.

Danny stood up and stared at the device in his hand and then looked at 84A as the creature raised its sword. In the background, he could see Kaia/

G'oth rising up behind 84A and forming a baseball bat. With his left hand, Danny pushed the button to activate the jammer…

…right as Kaia swung and caught 84A with every ounce of their combined strength, hitting the Togai in the back and sending it flying across the dish.

Without hesitation, Danny ran and stood under the white energy disc. When he was in position, he heaved the jammer at the disc and watched it disappear. Black tendrils wrapped around him and pulled him away just in time, as a blast of energy erupted from the tunnel and destroyed the area of the dish just below it. A few more seconds passed, and then it dissipated completely, along with the lightning that had been filling the air above the dish. The vibrations stopped as well, signaling that it was safe for Danny to put his hearing aid back in. "Thanks for the backup," he said, patting Kaia on the shoulder. "I wasn't expecting company out here."

"Hey, sorry I was late. Traffic. You know how it is. I had to use a Corvette for a shield."

"This night just keeps getting more heartbreaking."

A crashing noise arose from behind them, and turning to look, they watched as 84A staggered to his feet. The Togai looked around and saw that the quantum tunnel was gone, and its rage flared out of control. "No. No. NOOOOOOO! Foolish Earth creatures, do you have any idea what you've done? Do you?"

"We won," Kaia replied flatly.

"You have cut me off from home. My essence will not return to the crèche ever again. I am stranded on your festering pile of dirt. But you have not won."

Danny winked at the Togai. "Depends on where you're standing, I think."

"I am of the A designation, fools. I am the most powerful of us. And it is only through my dedication to the laws of my world that I do not use all of my skills within the sight of others. But others will never see me again, and I have no need to hide my gifts anymore."

Run! Run! Run!

"Oh come on. How bad can it – "

Before Kaia could react, dark brown tendrils flew out of 84A and wrapped themselves around her tightly. She and G'oth began to struggle, but she was held tight.

"But… but this is impossible…" Kaia blurted out. "It is forbidden by…"

The tendrils lifted her in the air. "As I said, I have had to hide the full extent of my gifts. No more."

With that, 84A slammed Kaia into the dish with all his might, causing her and G'oth to both cry out in pain. He then lifted her again, and slammed her down once more. He then slammed her into the nearest wall. Then the ground again, never letting go. The wall yet again. Danny, who had ran to the far side of the dish, watched in horror as the Togai tossed his friend around like a ragdoll. It was only when her screams stopped that the Togai dropped Kaia/G'oth's limp body to the ground.

"I will do the same to this wretched planet," 84A said in triumph.

Chapter 18
ARRIVAL PLUS 75 MINUTES:
A TANGLED WEB

84A surveyed the destruction he had caused since finally defeating the fugitive. Much of the structure where he had arrived on this world was now in ruin. The conveyances that had littered the outside were mostly smoking husks. Those Earth creatures that had previously survived had fled in terror of his power.

In all, he thought, his vengeance upon this planet was starting off rather well. Yet in his mind, he felt a sense of unease, as though something was not quite correct.

He decided to consider that issue later. For now, he would continue on.

Kaia? Can you hear me?

The young girl grunted something incomprehensible.

Please, Kaia, you must wake up.

"Aww, Mom… do I have to?" she said, unable to place where she was or who she was talking to.

I am not your parental unit, Kaia. It's G'oth.

"G'oth?" She paused to try and pull herself together. "What happened? Wait, I know what happened. We got a world-class beatdown."

Yes. We were both badly injured.

"Why aren't we dead? We should be dead, right?"

I was able to siphon power from lines beneath your radar dish. Using it, I healed us both. You more than I, obviously.

"How bad was I hurt?"

Legs, arms, pelvis, four ribs, two vertebrae… all broken.

"Healed or not, I should be hurting a lot worse than I am from that kind of smackdown."

I have deadened your pain centers. You will feel it… in the morning, I believe you would say.

"The Togai?"

The installation is destroyed. Your other Earthmen are hiding in the rocky area away from the dish, including Danny. The Togai is testing the limits of his power.

"We have to stop him. But I have no idea how. No way we can take that kind of punishment again."

I am at a loss.

"Nothing? No known weaknesses? They have to have something!" G'oth started to reply but she cut him off. "We know they aren't invincible!"

The Togai are born and bred to be hunters and warriors. They are like this from the moment they emerge from their crèche.

"Yeah, well, I was like this from the time I was born on the reservation, and I guess I am who I am, too. Hopeless little Hopi girl."

A silence passed between them. Suddenly, Kaia crawled to her knees and began to stand. "That's it! I know how to beat him!"

How?

"By using the two things I have that he doesn't."

Major Stewart moved his hands around the mental brick structure he had built around his consciousness, shielding him from 84A's prying eyes and ears. The creature still had control of his body, but thanks to the mental wall, it could not access his thoughts or memories.

"No information about troop numbers, weapons capabilities, nothing. You'll never get that stuff from me, you alien freak."

For the last fifteen minutes or so, by Stewart's count, the alien had been using its power, but not acting against anyone else. He could feel when they were in a true fight, but this felt more like a rampage. It was, the older man thought, unfortunate. He was not fully ready until now, but if the time arose again, and this thing found itself squaring off against someone who might be able to help him beat his captor?

Years of military discipline would be put to the test.

It did not take long, at full speed, for Kaia to spot 84A in the near distance. She could see the alien standing near the far entrance to the grounds, perhaps deciding which direction to take its destructive tendencies. "Hey! Stinky head!" she yelled as she approached. "We aren't done yet!"

84A whipped his body around, spotting Kaia/G'oth bearing down on him. "You! How?" With an angry howl, he flung a half dozen tendrils at Kaia, but this time, she dropped down into a slide and the tendrils flew past her overhead. As she slid, they formed their sword and sliced at the tendrils, severing two of them and causing 84A to cry out in pain as pieces of him dropped to the pavement.

"Not falling for it twice, dude," Kaia said, raising her sword as she saw him start to charge his. Taking a step forward, she swung down on 84A's sword, causing it to discharge its energy into the ground. With 84A's attention diverted, a third arm formed out of her right ribcage and punched mightily at 84A, hitting him in the jaw and dropping him to his knees.

"What? What was –"

Kaia used the third arm to hit him again. "That's called imagination, Mr. Togai," she said, forming a fourth arm from her left side, and punching him with that one as well. "I'm a human. I was born with an overabundance of it." She rained a series of blows down on him. "I think they left that out of your programming on Katahdin Prime."

Suddenly, one thick tendril emerged from 84A's midsection and rammed into Kaia's head, sending her sprawling backwards across the pavement. "You are right, Earth creature, I may not possess that quality. But I am exquisite at learning quickly."

Once again, they began trading blows, neither side gaining a true advantage over the other. After a couple of minutes passed, Kaia noticed that 84A had become so engaged in fighting her hand-to-hand that he had stopped charging his sword.

"It's now or never," she whispered, offering a silent prayer to the world. "Hey, Togai! You think you can conquer our world? You have no chance. We're a lot like you, you see. Grouped by our genetic characteristics. Tribal, if you will."

The alien stopped for a moment. "You are nothing

like me. Or any of my brethren on Katahdin Prime."

"My tribe," she continued, "are called the Hopi. Peaceful people. Imaginative. Did you know, we have our own myth about the birth and creation of the universe?"

"None may know the true origins of this universe, Earther."

She smiled. "The Hopi once believed that an enormous, powerful spider-woman gave birth to the universe and all that live in it." Kaia saw the Togai quivering and wondering what could be causing it. "Of course. I never believed in giant spiders… until now!"

In an instant, G'oth shifted himself around Kaia, forming the body of a giant spider as she pictured it in her mind. Caught off guard by the transformation, 84A hesitated, giving Kaia/G'oth time to shoot a wide black "web" from their chest and wrap around their foe as tight as they could.

A cry erupted from 84A as he began losing control of his shape. Kaia/G'oth held on as the alien writhed and snarled…

"Now!" Stewart yelled, summoning all of his will, and exploding the mental walls he had created, sending the fragments through the psychic bond 84A had forced upon him.

"YAAAAAAAAGGGGGGGGHHHHHHHH!" 84A screamed as Stewart fractured their bond from within. He lost control over his body for a moment, and Kaia/G'oth watched as part of him melted away and revealed Stewart.

"Whoever you are," the older man yelled, "do what you're going to do and do it quick!"

Kaia formed two "fangs" on the spider's head – fangs made of gun turrets – and chomped down on 84A's shoulder, biting him and sinking the fangs in deep. With no hesitation, they fired, sending the blast through 84A and tearing him away from Stewart's body.

Weakened and disrupted, 84A crawled away, barely maintaining coherency. "Thank you, Grandma," Kaia whispered as she shifted G'oth back to armor-mode and watched her foe try and gather himself

"I don't know what to do now," she said. "I'm not a killer."

Yet he cannot be allowed to –

SHHHHHHUNNNNNNK!

Kaia was snapped out of her reverie by the sound of Major Stewart using 84A's sword to cut the Togai in half.

"Thanks for letting me finish it, kid. I owed him one," the older man said in a gravelly voice.

She looked at him blankly for a moment, then nodded. "Yes, sir. Totally my plan there, sir."

He gave her a warm smile, looking at the armor surrounding her body. "Hmm. Well, long night. What say you get out of here before backup finally shows, call it a day?"

"Yes, sir."

Stewart winked at her. "We'll talk again someday."

Chapter 19
ARRIVAL PLUS 1 DAY:
ACCESSORIZING

Kaia was awoken by a gentle tap from her mother. "Good morning, sleepyhead."

She gave a long yawn and fluttered her eyes as she adjusted to the light of day. "Hey, mom. Wassup? Why are you getting me up so early?"

Her mother laughed. "Early? It's noon!"

"Noon? Oh, wow… guess I was tired."

Lilith smiled at her daughter. "I guess you were. You even left your hair-tie in when you went to bed."

"Uhh… science will do that to you, I guess."

The older woman sat back and shook her head. "You know, sometimes I think you might be crazy with all this science stuff. I think about it, and I think about how no one in our family has ever been so obsessed with their education as you are." She paused and looked skyward. "Sometimes I even wonder how you're my daughter." Kaia looked at her, shocked. "But then I realize that is exactly what does make you my daughter. You don't have to be anyone but yourself, and that's good enough. I'm proud of you."

Kaia threw her arms around her mother's neck. "Thank you, mom."

"I'm also proud of you because you washed and gassed up the truck. Don says thanks, by the way."

"Seemed like the right thing to do."

"I'll start some lunch. Grab a shower and join the world, kiddo."

Kaia stood in front of the bathroom mirror and watched as G'oth unwound from her hair and moved down to her arm, forming a bracelet.

What happens now?

She started the water. "Cleaning up. Lunch. Then…"

"The whole wide world is ours."

S.E.T.I. Alpha Six shimmered under the Australian sky, the stars unblemished by light pollution. Inside the installation's control room, the scientists in charge moved with purpose as they prepared to put the dish online.

"Remember, no mistakes. Keep an eye on all readouts. Let's show the Americans how it's done!"

Power surged through the dish and it fired its signal toward the heavens. The crew watched as all seemed to be perfect. However, the perfection did not last. "Sir, we're reading unusual power levels. Something weird is…"

A crash of thunder erupted above the dish, and bolts of lightning began criss-crossing the surface. Astonished, the scientists watched as a strange disc of white energy appeared directly over the dish…

…and then S.E.T.I. Alpha Six went offline.

Never… the End!

ABOUT THE AUTHOR

Marc Mason is an author and a college professor based in Tempe, Arizona. His other works include SCHISM: OUT OF THE SHADOWS, THE JOKER'S ADVOCATE, THE AISLE SEAT: LIFE ON THE EDGE OF POPULAR CULTURE, and RED SONJA: RAVEN. He is the owner and editor-in-chief of The Comics Waiting Room (cwr.comicswaitingroom.com), and broadcasts his thoughts on life at MarcMason.com and via Twitter (@marcmason).

ABOUT THE CREATOR

Shannon Eric Denton is an award winning storyteller. Shannon created ACTIONOPOLIS to actualize his ideas into a line of fast paced books for adventure lovers of any age. He has been fortunate to have worked professionally as an artist, writer, editor, director, and producer making comic books, children's books, Emmy nominated TV shows, Oscar nominated movies, toys and video games for studios such as Marvel, DC, Disney, WB, Fox, Lego, Sony, Nickelodeon, and Cartoon Network.

www.shannondenton.com
www.actionopolis.com
www.agentofdanger.com

ACTIONOPOLIS:
When Adventure Is Your Destination!

Other books from
ACTIONOPOLIS & *AGENT of D.A.N.G.E.R.*

- Agent of D.A.N.G.E.R.
- All Robots Must Die
- The Anubis Tapestry
- Astro-Aces
- Blacke's Loch
- Blackfoot Braves Society
- Children of Olympus
- Dragonblood
- Evolver
- Exo-Bio
- The Forest King
- Gargantuan
- Heir to Fire
- Henrietta Hex
- Inheritance
- Last of the Lycans
- Legend of Tigerfist
- Master of Voodoo
- Megamatrix
- Me/2
- Monstrous
- The Nightmare Expeditions
- Prototype
- Reckers
- Royal Crown Mystery Detectives League
- Schism
- Spirit of the Samurai

- Sword of the Seas
- Toltec
- ThunderBreakers
- Upgrader 2
- Valkyra
- Vampirium
- What I Did On My Hypergalactic Interstellar Summer Vacation
- White Knight
- Winged Victory
- Wonderworld
- Zombie Monkey Monster Jamboree

And Many More Titles Coming Soon!

A multitude of Adventures await!
Available as either physical manifestations...
a printed masterpiece on paper...or as a
program in the matrix for the technologically
advanced who prefer a digital eBook format!
You can find all the Actionopolis titles in print
or available on your preferred
eReading device!

WWW.ACTIONOPOLIS.COM

www.ingramcontent.com/pod-product-compliance
Lightning Source LLC
Chambersburg PA
CBHW030631130626
46552CB00002B/800